T0365368

Order this book online at www.trafford.com
or email orders@trafford.com

Most Trafford titles are also available at major online book retailers.

Print information available on the last page.

ISBN: 978-1-4907-6287-6 (sc)
        978-1-4907-6288-3 (e)

Because of the dynamic nature of the Internet, any web addresses or links contained in this book may have changed
since publication and may no longer be valid. The views expressed in this work are solely those of the author and do not
necessarily reflect the views of the publisher, and the publisher hereby disclaims any responsibility for them.

Our mission is to efficiently provide the world's finest, most comprehensive book publishing service, enabling every author to experience
success. To find out how to publish your book, your way, and have it available worldwide, visit us online at www.trafford.com

Any people depicted in stock imagery provided by Thinkstock are models,
and such images are being used for illustrative purposes only.
Certain stock imagery © Thinkstock.

Trafford rev. 09/09/2015

 www.trafford.com

North America & international
toll-free: 1 888 232 4444 (USA & Canada)
fax: 812 355 4082

The Great Squirrel Rebellion

Gowon Fisher

This book is dedicated to all the woodland creatures,

who on lessons of life, are often our best teachers.

G.M.F.

The Great Squirrel Rebellion

Gowon M. Fisher

Buzz buzz hummed the bees,

as they zipped through the brush,

sipping nectar from flowers, of

violet, and blush.

Hop hop went the rabbits,

as they frolicked with ease,

enjoying the calm, of the soft summer breeze.

Cheer cheer sang the birds in the leaves of the trees,
filling valley and meadow with bright melodies.

A deer in the meadow,

looked up at the sky, his quiet companion

an orange butterfly.

But deep in the forest in an old sycamore,

dwelt a family of squirrels getting angry and sore.

Why were they angry you ask?

At the end of the woods, stood a tiny house,

inside lived a woman named Griselda Grouse.

She had a bird feeder which she filled every day,

and all the birds would come eat, sing and play.

Racy red cardinals, a blue jay or two,

a king fisher cloaked in a vibrant hue.

A crooning robin, a sparrow painted dun,

nibbling on seed, under the warm morning sun.

Mrs. Grouse seems a kind sort, without malice or spite.

Well, if you're a squirrel, beg to differ, you might.

To her, the squirrels were pests.

They were most unwelcome guests.

Their presence made her glower.

Her face and words turned sour.

Her temper like an asp.

Her voice a fearsome rasp.

She scolded, she chided, she fussed and she fumed.

She shook her fist angrily, and thud went the broom.

"You rats with tails!" she angrily railed.

"You furry thieves!" she hissed and seethed.

"You pillaging pipsqueaks with beady eyes!

Leave my seed alone, go eat some flies!"

All her warnings, the squirrels did not heed,

so she mixed some hot peppers in with the seed.

Then watched from the window with a gleeful gaze,

as the squirrels breathed out, a red hot blaze.

But Mr. Squirrel soon foiled her devious plot,
with lots of insect friends, who loved their peppers hot.

But Miss Grouse quickly blew her top.

She vowed the squirrels would have to stop.

She hung the feeder in mid air,

and dared the squirrels to reach it there.

Mr. Squirrel and his son came to feed the next day,

and saw the new obstacle that was put in their way.

"It looks rather risky." said Mr. Squirrel with a sigh.

"I'm not scared," said his son, "I'll give it a try."

"I'm about to jump, so wish me luck.

Oh No! Oh No! I think I'm stuck!"

Luckily, Mr. Squirrel pulled him to safety.

"Next time my boy, let's not be so hasty."

But Mr. Squirrel with his quick thinking brain,

found a way to get seed without any pain.

He called his cousin, a flying squirrel,

who was the highest flyer in the whole squirrel world.

Zoom zoom went his cousin as he soared over hills,

and performed daring feats that gave other squirrels chills.

He leapt to the feeder with grace and ease,

and gathered as much food as he pleased.

Then flew back to the forest with his cheeks full of seed,

and passed it around to all those in need.

Now Miss Grouse was mad as a hornet.

"Those squirrels heard my warning but dared to ignore it!

I'll teach those varmints to judge me a fool!

I'll set the feeder adrift in the pool!"

Griselda giggled as she built a raft.

"Squirrels can't swim, heh heh" she laughed.

31

But Mr. Squirrel wasn't deterred by water or wood,

because squirrels **can** swim, and they swim pretty good!

He dove in the pool with a splash and a splish,

swimming as well as a school of fish.

He swam and he swam the entire length,

and just about used up all his strength.

But still got his seed, whether she liked it or not.

He proved that persistence can foil any plot.

At this, Miss Grouse was full of gall,

and came up with a plan to rival them all.

She placed her two cats near the bird feeder,

to menace the squirrels, especially their leader.

"Beware!" hissed the cats, their teeth sharp as knives.

The squirrels took one look, and ran for their lives.

"We cannot fight cats, we can only run.

It seems Miss Grouse has finally won."

"Don't despair!" said Mr. Squirrel, "There's still much to do."

"But if our plan is to work, I'll need all of you.

Now think hard my friends. Clear your head of the fog.

Every cat fears the bark of a dog!"

"Brilliant idea!" applauded the other squirrels,

as they danced and jumped and joyfully twirled.

"ARF, ARF!" was the sound heard throughout the forest,

for the squirrels had created a canine chorus.

When they were quite certain they'd perfected their bark,

they crept back to the feeder, although it was dark.

On the porch the cats were all fast asleep,

the squirrels snuck behind them without making a peep.

"ARF ARF!" They all barked with all their might,

and the two nasty cats ran away in fright.

Miss Grouse was awakened by a loud pitter, patter,

what she saw out her window made her madder and madder.

She seethed and she steamed like a fire-breathing dragon,

the squirrels were escaping with her seeds in their wagon!

She ran outside, ready for a duel,

but she lost her footing, and fell in the pool!

Meanwhile, all the squirrels

were enjoying their treasure.

They munched and they nibbled

with zeal and real pleasure.

But Mr. Squirrel piped up

before his next bite.

"Something's wrong," he announced,

"something isn't quite right."

"But we have seed," answered the squirrels,

"what more do we need?"

"It's true," Mr. Squirrel, responded,

we have enough seed."

"But the birds now have nothing,

because of our greed!"

The other squirrels said, "What you say is very true.

But after all, really,

what else can we do?"

Each one knew the answer,

in their hearts, each one knew...

47

So they put down the seed, although it was hard,

and made their way back to Griselda's yard.

And standing in the yard, her clothes sopping wet,

was Griselda Grouse and her frightened pet.

Miss Grouse opened her mouth wide to speak.

Her voice was neither whisper nor shriek.

"You squirrels steal seed from the birds,

and always make such a mess.

You know I am telling the truth,

so don't deny it, confess!"

"We're sorry." said Mr. Squirrel, with a bashful smile.

"Were sorry," said the others, "We were wrong by a mile!"

Then Miss Grouse thought. She thought for a while.

"I'm sorry too," said Miss Grouse.

"Perhaps I was harsh with no need,

but promise me there'll be less mess."

and maybe I'll give you some seed,

"We promise!" said the squirrels, "There'll be no more mess!"

"We promise!" they repeated, **"We aim to impress!"**

So the squirrels were given seed,

and committed no further misdeed.

Griselda's temper softened,

and flared up far less often.

One night after supper
Mr. Squirrel posed two questions:
"Now what have we learned?
What valuable lesson?"

And...

In the calm of the forest that night,
the squirrels in a chorus unite.
**"There's no reason to fight,
and no reason to shout.
It's always much better
to talk everything out!"**

The End

Vocabulary

asp   a snake

blush   light pink color

chided   to scold

companion   a friend or pal

deterred   to discourage

devious   sneaky

dun   a grayish–brown color

dwelt   to live in

frolicked   to run, jump and play

gall   a feeling of irritation

Vocabulary

glower	an angry look
hue	a tint or shade of a color
malice	wanting to do harm
persistence	to keep trying
pillaging	to steal
rasp	scratchy
seethe	bubbling over with anger
spite	to be mean
sycamore	a kind of tree
varmint	a small animal
zeal	full of excitement

Printed in the United States
By Bookmasters